# Cyril and Pat

## Emily Gravett

TW🦉 HOOTS

Lake Park only had one Squirrel,
All alone and sad (poor Cyril).

Until the morning he met Pat,
His new best friend, a big grey . . .

Pat and Cyril spent each day
Thinking up good games to play.

They liked to put on puppet shows,
And test how fast a skateboard goes.

Their *favourite* games were Hide-and-seek,

And one that they called Pigeon Sneak.

Shhh

Oh Cyril, can't you see that your friend Pat
Is not like you. Your friend's a . . .

Real joker!

At lunchtime, when the ducks were fed,
Pat jumped in and took some bread.

Oh Cyril, can't you see that your friend Pat
Is not like you. Your friend's a . . .

And when they both got chased by Slim,
Together they outwitted him.

Slim Ⓢ – – – – –
Pat Ⓟ ·········
Cyril Ⓒ – – – –

Oh Cyril,
  can't you see that your friend Pat
Is not like you. Your friend's a . . .

CLEVER SQUIRREL,
And you can't catch us!

shouted Cyril.

Pat tried to learn to earn a treat
Like Cyril could, by looking sweet.

But no one threw a treat for Pat.

Urgh! Mum,
I saw a great big . . .

Oh Cyril, can't you see that your friend Pat
Is nothing but a dirty rat?

Oh Cyril, can't you see that your friend Pat
Is nothing but a *thieving* rat?

Oh Cyril, can't you see it? Facts are facts.
SQUIRRELS CAN'T BE FRIENDS WITH RATS!

Cyril, now back on his own,
Tried to play their games alone.

But when he tried to outrun Slim,
Things didn't go so well for him.

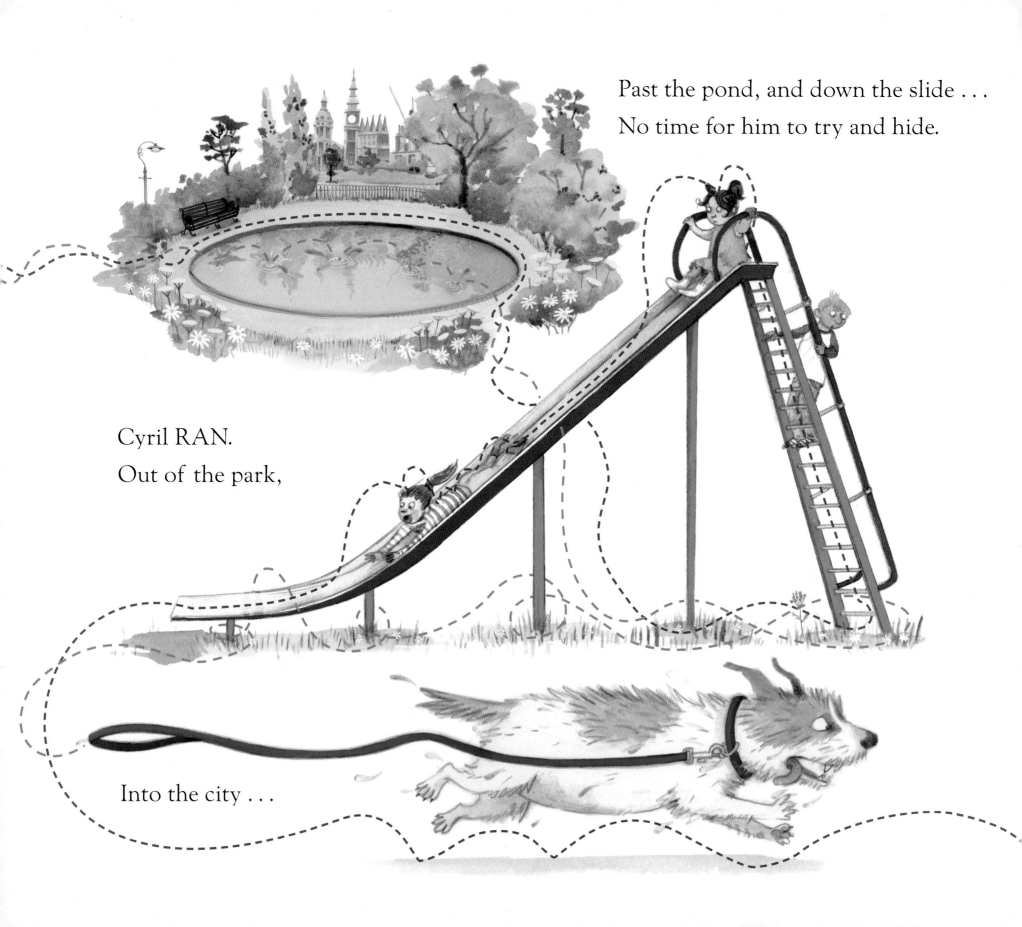

Past the pond, and down the slide . . .
No time for him to try and hide.

Cyril RAN.
Out of the park,

Into the city . . .

into the dark.

All alone and scared.
(Poor Cyril.)

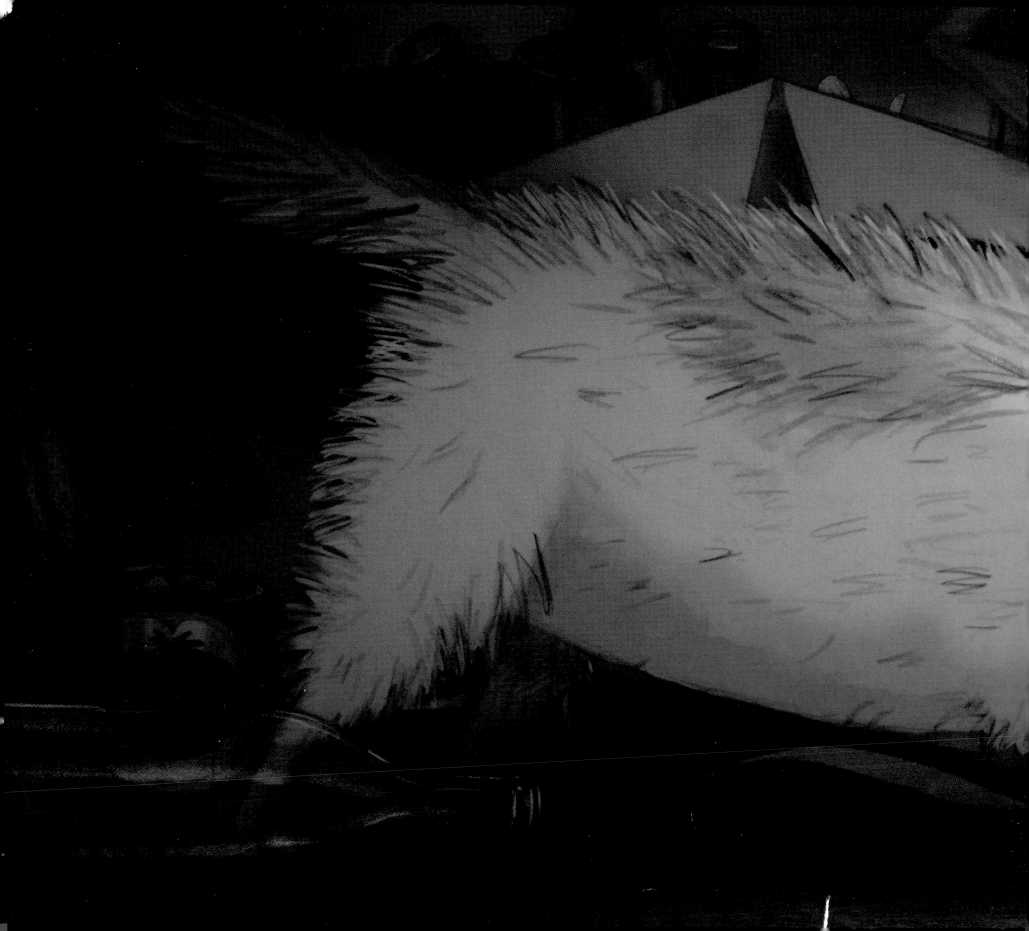

Not *quite* alone, you stupid squirrel.
And *not so brave* without that rat.

"Ahem. Do you mean ME?" said Pat.

Lake Park still only has one squirrel –
But he is not alone. Now Cyril
Lives there with a large grey rat,
His brave and clever best friend, Pat.

First published 2018 by Two Hoots
an imprint of Pan Macmillan

20 New Wharf Road, London N1 9RR

Associated companies throughout the world
www.panmacmillan.com

ISBN: 978-1-5098-5727-2

The illustrations in this book were created
using pencil and watercolour.

www.twohootsbooks.com

1 3 5 7 9 8 6 4 2
A CIP catalogue record for this book
is available from the British Library.

Printed in China

For Merry